VOYAGE OF A LETHAL PATRIOT

ABIK DEY (GUWAHATI | ASSAM)

Made with ♥ on the Notion Press Platform
www.notionpress.com

I dedicate this book to my closest friend Parvati Dey for sticking it out with me, Thank you for still being with me.

I would also like to dedicate it to my family for supporting me and my two friends, Sujata Das and Arpana Bhowal for their support and their undying friendship to me.

Contents

Disclaimer   *vii*

Preface   *ix*

Acknowledgements   *xi*

1. Who I Am   1

2. Turning Point   7

3. Training Phase   9

4. Lily   12

Disclaimer

This is a fictional based story. So, all the characters and actions in this book are Authors own imagination. And here in this story "Author" refers to **RAJ**, who is the main character of this story. The views and opinions are expressed in this book are purely of the author's and not of any government body or agency, publisher, or Assam police. The book is published to only for the people to know about the brave officers who are giving everything for the nation without any personal interest, unknowingly and anonymously protecting us from various enemies.

Preface

" Voyage Of A Lethat Patriot " Is The first Edition Written By The Author Abik Dey. It's A Fictional Novel, Describing The Journey Of a Secret agent

In this book there was a story and Raj is the main character of this story and the story is Beautifully Described by the author, The Journey Of a secret agent From His Childhood Days.

Raj First get into the work in a intelligence agency after that he was promoted into a higher rank.

Author Have Potray How Brave Secret Agents manage their Personal life as well as professional life anonymously.

Hope This Book Will make All The Readers and Country's Citizens Proud.

Author: Abik Dey

Acknowledgements

This book would never have been possible without my two friends, who supported me in this journey of my writing.

I would like to thank my closest friend Parvati Dey for helping me to write this book and making her own contribution. My brother and my parents supplied their memories as well as their support. The information which Arpana Bhowal and Sujata Das provided me that was invaluable.

We worked for this book in a variety of places. None matched the comfort at my sweet home, and the table there I worked continuously.

CHAPTER ONE

Who I Am

_Me:_

Every story has a starting.

Mine started in Nagaon, Assam. I was born in a middle-class family in Nagaon, middle part of ASSAM. I was the elder son of my parents. I grew up in a small town where I learned the importance of family and traditional values, like patriotism, self-reliance, and watching out for family and neighbours. I still tried to live my life according to those values. I had a strong sense of justice because I thought that it is very important to protect others. I was raised with and I still believed in the Hindu faith. My family had a deep faith in god. My parents always taught me about the stories related god. Ramayana, Gita, Mahabharata, Bible, Quran were those books from where my mom dad used to tell me about gods of different religions. If I had to order my priorities then that would be: Country, God and Family. There might be some debate on where those last two falls – those days I had come around to believe that family may, under some circumstances, out rank country. It's a close race. I always tried to give my first priority to my country then my family then others.

But yes I also liked to spend some times of the day in the district library; the environment of the library was very peaceful for me. Whenever I entered to the library I was feeling something too good, so I tried to visit that place once a day not only for reading but also for keeping my mind fresh. The librarian sir also used to encourage me to read books. And I often visited his home to return the books because the opening time of the library was 10:30 AM, but my school started at 10 AM. So, I used to visit his home for returning the books. I could never forget those days when I visited to his home and he always offered me snacks. He really loved me a lot.

At the same moment, I liked to have fun because I thought life is too short.

My Father:

My father worked for a private medicine company in the north-eastern region of India. He was not in a manager post, means he was not in a high post. He was just an employee who worked for day and night only for us. He was not unhappy with his job because for him the job which he was doing was the reason behind our food which were getting. He got many offers from various multi-national companies, which were 10 times more salary than the job what he was doing at that time. If he wanted, he could have accepted any of them but the strange thing was that he had not done. One day I asked him, "Why aren't you accepting these offers which make you more successful". He smiled and replied me "I don't care how much money I get, it's not worth it if I am not happy to doing it". That's the most valuable piece of advice he ever gave me. After a few days when he came from work, I asked him again a bunch of question relating to my future, like what stream I had to choose after my 10th, what would be the attitude to be successful in life? He answered me in just one sentence "Do whatever you want in your life. I can just Sharp you, the job of cutting is yours". Literally I just noted that on my dairy.

My father was not simple, I never saw such a hard working person, the respect for his job, the disciplinary attitude, and everything was not ordinary. For me my father was my first superhero of my life before all the television's superheroes. I had always love toy guns, which my father gave me every year in the occasion of *DURGA PUJA* until I become fourteen (14) years old.

My father's views or opinions on God were a little different from others (including my mom), he believed "God will not help you if you prayed day and night in the temple; God will only help you if you work hard and keep your family happy". I never saw him to go to any temple, if my mom told him "No need to go to work today I am going to temple so you also have to go with me". Without thinking anything he told her that "Sorry I can't come with you". Because for him, God is in our heart not in any individual temple or in any individual place.

In my school days I didn't have any friend because I was an introvert type of guy but still I never felt alone only because of my father. He was too friendly with me. But at the same time he was able to combine that with a good dose of fatherly discipline. There was a line between us and i never wanted to cross that. I got my share of whipping (punishment) when I deserved that, but not too excessive and never in anger.

My Brother:

Me and my brother always wanted to have some fun but we just stopped when we heard the sound of the cycle's chain which was coming in front of us. We became silent because when he came from his duty or work or from some tours we just gave him a few minutes to calm down.

We went to school together because our school was a little far away from our home. So my mom always told me to hold his hand until we reach the school. My brother was 4 years younger than me but he could give as good as he got, and he would never give up. He's tongue in cheek character and one of my closest friends of those days. We gave each other hell, but we also had a lot of fun and always knew we had each other's back. One day without telling anyone he went to our grandma's house. The distance of our grandma's house is 200 metres away from our home. At 1:30PM my mom told us loudly "Raj come to the dining room and has your lunch and yes also ask your brother that will he eat now or later". Then I started looking for him but I couldn't find him. After that I told my mother "Mom bro is not at home where is he?" After hearing this she got very scared. As time passed our tension was growing continuously after 1 hour she told me to call the police. After 2 hours of registering missing complaint, we got a call from my grandma's house that my brother went to their home without knowing anyone. This incidents remind us about his childhood witch. We really missed those days but yes remembering those days always helped me to smile.

My Mother:

My mother, My Mom, I never saw any woman whose efforts for her child like my mom. She was just an amazing woman who could do anything means just anything for her family and children. I couldn't describe about her in few lines. It is just impossible for anyone not only me to describe her\his mother. My mom was too much hard working. She was the only member of our home who woke up before all of us and slept after all of us. She always support me in every walk of my life irrespective the situation: Good, Bad, critical, etc.

When I was preparing for my HSLC examination, I always go to bed between 4 to 5AM she woke up near 3:30AM and made breakfast for me without a single sound, she thought that if she made any sound I would be disturbed so she made breakfast silently. When I went to keep my book on my book shelf, she called me from the dining room because my book shelf was near to kitchen. After completing my breakfast, I used to go to sleep. But not my mom, she started her daily routine. Max to max she slept for only 4 to 5 hours which was not sufficient for a human being. She was not an ordinary woman she was something different, something extra ordinary. Normally I ate with my mother at night means in dinner she sat with me at the same dining table, at first she served me all dishes which she made and at last she gave a homemade mango pickle which was just incomparable. I really love and respect her so much I can't express but I really love her. I always thank my God to give me mom like her and dad like him.

My School Day:

School days were another memorable time in my life. My journey in my school life started at the age of 3. I was too flickering so my parents thought of admitting me to a school. I was the kind of student who always wanted to keep myself in the teacher's good book and I was too. I was very polite to everyone. I loved to keep myself in discipline because I was very clear that without discipline I am not going to be successful or do anything great in my life. I was not a very gifted or intelligent student; I was just an average student whose limit end at 85%. The love and guidance that I have received from my respected teacher is very precious and the knowledge that I have received from teachers are the reasons which are still helping me to make my career. I am deeply grateful to all my teachers (gurus).

CHAPTER TWO

Turning Point

My life took a big turn on the day 3rd July 2018.That was a normal day like every day. But I was wrong because something happened on that day what I never imagined. Every day at 5AM my dad went to the railway station to buy newspaper. After buying the newspaper he came back to home and gave the newspaper to my paternal uncle. After he completed the reading he gave that to my dad. After he completed his reading at last the newspaper was given to me by my dad. I became late because at that period of time I woke up between 6:30 to 6:45 AM. At 7 AM I gave my little amount of time to read the newspaper. As per my daily routine like every day, I was reading the newspaper. But when my reading was going to complete then I noticed a strange thing in the last page of the newspaper. It was an advertisement but I was not able to understand anything because the language of that advertisement was different that was not English. I asked my dad what was written there. He replied in an awkward face "why are you just wasting your time in such advertisement? I have told you to read all the headlines and choose some of the report which is informative for you. " But I was too much curious about the advertisement so, I started to search on the Google for two days without knowing any member of my family. After two days of hard research I found a result. As I was thinking something interesting, my probability was come true. After seeing the result I was just shocked because that was an advertisement for a much respected service of our country. In Morse language, there was written that, 'if anyone wants to serve for the country without any personal interest then he/she can apply for the post and those who are interested can fill the form and just sent it to this number ****.' Without thinking anything I just send all my details on that number. After 4 days I got SMS, in that SMS they provide me some information. I have requested to give 100 marks exam after 30 days and I got 7 e-books through given link. I thoroughly read the entire book one by one. This was the first time when I studied very seriously and hardly. After 30 days the day came when I had to give the exam. I was nervous but my nervousness vanished after 1 hour of giving the exam. After 7 days I received an SMS, in that SMS they provided me a link. When I opened that link, my happiness was in heaven. My feeling at that time was such that I have achieved everything. After seeing my result, I was really very happy because I worked really hard for that exam. After 1 day i got another SMS where i had to fill all my details like my score of exam, rank and everything. After filling everything and tapping on submit icon, I received an OTP which I had to fill on that link after clicking on submit icon. After waiting for 4 days I got a mail where they were appointing in my hometown as I was a student at that time but I had to go through a tough training before I was appointed.

Training Phase

In my training phase my biggest challenge was going to outside without knowing anyone of my family and returned from there without knowing anyone. I had to wake up at 3:30 AM. and a car always waited for me from 3:15 AM, and the car took me to our training zone. After reaching theret hey served us breakfast, after completing our breakfast our commander ordered us for running practice which was approximately 5KM of running practice. After that We went to the indoor training hall where our martial art teacher trained us different types of martial art. The main martial art was krav maga which was developed by Israel Defence Forces (IDF), it is derived from a combination of techniques used in Aikido, Judo, Karate, Boxing and Wrestling. It is known for its focus on real-world situations media footage demonstrating krav maga techniques to deal with assailants in mok combat using multiple different types of weapons; named a pole, a knife, gun, a rifles and hand-to-hand.

After 1 hour of our martial arts training we got orders to go to the shooting hall for shooting practice. That was my favourite phase of my daily training as I was obsessed with toy guns and rifles since childhood. So after getting in real I really fell in love with them. Whenever I saw those

Glock-17 pistols, a variety of Russian, American assault rifles etc. But yes at first I really felt very tired and severe pain in my hand. But as the days passed by, my pain and all types of problems that I was facing at first became less with time.

????? ??? ??????????:

When our commander shouted in full force "Come to the ground." If anyone would not come, after calling more than 2 times, he would be punished, the punishment included 100 push-ups, 10 km run etc. I was also punished by our commander. My punishment was that I had to run 1 km in 2 minutes. If I couldn't, I would have run 20KM. I got punished just because my shoes were not cleaned properly.

After 7 months of hard training, I was able to handle all serious situations. I was totally prepared by mentally and physically, luckily my mom dad never got any clue what I was doing they didn't even know that I daily went outside of the house.

The day came when an officer of RAW came to the headquarters to deliver our service. We were total 4 members of that year. Everyone got their service and posting except me. I was very nervous; he checked my reports for 30 minutes. After that he told me "Why are you here?" I replied him that "I am here to do something for our motherland". After seeing all the details of my training phase, He offered me another service which was a higher rank from that. Without thinking anything I directly accepted his proposal. On that service I met many brave and brilliant officers' .Everyone was very nice with me but one of them became my good friend, we called her Miss. BOSE. We had done many operations together. That's how I started my journey in this field.

Probably at the age of 16-17 I saw many things which people could only imagine. In our boot camp I was the youngest and the most senior rank officer. When other officers used to call me 'Sir', my reaction in my mind was like – hihihihihi.

Now I really miss those days with my training colleagues.

My regrets are about the people I couldn't save – many civilians, soldiers, my buddies. I still feel their loss. I still ache for my failure to protect them.

CHAPTER FOUR

Lily

Everything was going well; I had balanced my professional life as well as my private life. At that time I had three closest friends they were like my family members. Their names were Adi Jaiswal, Jaan Joshi, and my best friend Bipasha Das. We were total four friends. Our friendship was different from the others. Every week we planned to visit different places and every Saturday we went to that place. One day we made plan to go outside in the western part of our district. Next day we went out as per our plan. After one hour of our journey we took a stoppage after 23 KM for lunch. After our lunch, we had decided to click some photographs above the flyover because we saw a picturesque view of nature from that flyover, mixture of beautiful scenery and mountains. Adi had a DSLR camera so; he was taking beautiful photos of us and also the magnificent scenario. And while taking such pictures, Adi saw a girl and called me, "Raj! Come here. Look at the girl who was wearing school uniform. She is so pretty, isn't she? "Then I told him," Where? There are many girls here who wearing school uniform. But how do I know which girl you are talking about? "Then he told me to see near a tree on the school's playground. Then I noticed her. He saw her from the flyover because the school was below the flyover.

Adi was just jumping after seeing that girl. I told him, "May I call her and introduce you." He just said 'no'. From that day every Saturday after our school we went to that place to saw that girl but I only went with them to seeing the beautiful view of nature and to feel the place, that place was too peaceful. I was just obsessed with that place because that gave me peace and tranquillity. As the days passed, Adi's love for that girl was growing. But unfortunately Adi didn't know her name, class, age etc. But day by day he just became mad on that girl. But one day i went to ask Adi, "When you will go home? I have to go because I have some tasks at home which I have to complete within a day". And suddenly I saw a girl with Adi's crush. She was playing with her in the playground. After seeing her, my reaction was just,"Wowwwwww how beautiful she is!" I couldn't take my eyes off her. So I called Adi and asked him, "Do you know that girl who is playing with your crush?" After that Adi laughed at me and replied me in a funny face, "What a silly question; I don't even know my crush's name then how can you think that I know the name of my crush's friend". And after that Adi told Bipasha and Jaan, "Have you seen Raj;I don't know what happened with him, he had been staring at my crush's friend for a long time and also asked me about her. I think maybe he likes her. What do you both think?" Then Jaan and Bipasha replied, okay! Then we ask him what is going on in his mind. After that they asked me, "Raj! What happened to you? Why are you looking at that girl so much?" Then I told them, "Oh dude; There is no such special thing, that's why I asked because that girl is looking very beautiful and nothing much." After that we went to our home. But I don't know why I couldn't forget that girl. Day by day i was curious about that girl. So I decided to go to that place without knowing anyone. And next Thursday

I went to that place and saw her again. I don't know why I couldn't take my eyes off her. I clicked a photo of her and went to our headquarter to give the photo to our cyber cell to take all information about her. In few moments I got all the details of her. Her name was Lily and she was a local girl of that place. Don't know why I was becoming mad on Lily. And from then whenever we went to that place; I always used to see Lily. One day Jaan, Bipasha and Adi asked me, "Are you fall in love with Lily?" I just said, no I don't love her. I just want to be a good friend of her. But one day when I saw Lily with a male friend doesn't know why I was feeling too much jealous. I called my assistant (Miss Bose) and told her "I am sending a photo of a guy. Give me the full detail of him within 10 minutes and yes also tell me the relation between him and Lily". After 10 minutes she told me that "Sir; they are classmates and their relation is only brother and sister". Don't know why I was feeling good after listening everything from Miss Bose.

Days were passing. After 7 months suddenly we had to face a disastrous pandemic, for the pandemic government imposed an emergency named lockdown where every citizen had to stay at their house. All industries, business, school, colleges were closed. So for that no one had the right to went out of their house without any valid reason. First lockdown was too strict, that's why we weren't allowed to going out of our homes. But not for me I had the pass to go anywhere so my life was going normal.

After few months when all the lockdown was cancelled again we started to go to that place to seeing Adi's crush but I used to go to see Lily. After few months we all got our exam routine so we stopped to go there.

After few months when our exam finished and now we all had to choose our college where we want to take admission. But our aim was that where Adi's crush would take admission, we would also take there.

Now I was finding the detail. After some days we got information that she took admission in a college which was near to our house. So, me and my 3 friends directly took admission at that college. After 2 weeks our college authorities opened some groups where the entire students were separated into Science and arts stream. Because of the pandemic our college started classes in online. Now Adi and his crush were in the same class, same stream and same section. IN our college sections were divided in the behalf of their medium and both Adi and his crush took admission in English medium. So through that group Adi got her number, now they were classmate. So he texted her but her phone was not actually her so she didn't reply to Adi. She used her mother's phone. As days were passed Adi was continuously trying to impress her. One day he told her that he love her. But unfortunately she directly rejected him without thinking anything. Adi felt very bad. Adi was thinking that I had everything: money, power, house, car, etc. And he was also a good guy so no one ever rejected him. Adi's father was a big business tycoon of our nation; Adi's total net worth was 780 million. From his childhood his father provided him everything which he want irrespective the cost. He couldn't accept her rejection, so he went to England for his studies and tried to forget everything and my friend Jaan Joshi; she was Adi's sister, she also went to London with Adi.

I was in Arts stream and in our college Arts stream's online class started after few weeks from science. I had done my first class in online which was not too bad but it would have been better if our first class started from the classroom I mean in offline. After one week one day our political sir told us to switch on our camera to give an introduction. After that two students gave their introduction and also a girl who opened her camera, again I saw lily, I was just jumped from the bed and opened my college group and started to searching for her number. After 1 minute I found her number. Now I got surety that Lily was in my class and in my section. Next day I had to go to Bangalore for an official meeting. So I just forgot about her because of my work load. From Bangalore I had to go to Indian Military Academy (IMA) Dehradun for training. After that I also had to go to Nahan, Himachal Pradesh in the school of Special Forces. After 14 days when I was returning to home in the middle of the road my driver told me that he had some private work. I just told him that ok then parked the car near that colony. I would wait there. When i was waiting for my driver inside the car I noticed Lily with Adi's crush and her brother at that colony. And then I checked Lily's profile again and her profile picture. She looked so beautiful in that dress. I was looking at her, my eyes were not moving from her photo. Then I thought to give her a message but could not give. And I spent my whole day just seeing her profile picture. Next day again I joined my online class, I again got chance to listen her voice. In the afternoon first time I gave her a text through whatsapp. That was the first time when I texted a girl from myself. She replied me but she got disturbed because I texted her during her class. That's why she told me that we would talk after my class was over. I said, Okay. After that when her class was over, I texted her again. She started thinking, Ohh God! How *chipku* he is! And since then we started talking and i found out that yesterday was her birthday. And then this thought came to my mind, if I had texted her yesterday, I would have wished her a very happy birthday too. As days were passed, our conversation started slowly. But at first she was not feeling comfortable with me. First few day's conversation was not too good. Gradually we became very good friends. A few days later, when our college was about to open, in the evening I got a very bad news that my best friend Bipasha was in the hospital. Immediately I went to the hospital and I asked her parents, "What happened uncle-aunty, why are you admitting her to the hospital?" Her mother was crying loudly then her father replied to me in a very low voice "Bipasha is suffering from cancer since last one year, she is in the final stage and doctor told us that she doesn't have enough time". After listening to everything, I could not understand anything; I just sat on a chair of the hospital. After 2 hours Bipasha's father touched my shoulder and told me "Raj! Go back to your home". When I looked at the clock on the wall, it was 11 o'clock in the night; I did not know how I spent 2 hours in that chair.

The next day our college opened, after reaching the college I got a message from Bipasha's father that she was no more. I had controlled my emotion whole day. That day I didn't talk to anyone of my class, till Lily told me that the first day of your college you just ignored me. But only I knew how I manage my emotion whole day. We sometimes started talking in Leisure. As the days passed I became normal only because of Lily. One day after college was over; Lily asked me, "Are you going home from here? I said, "No, I am going to my coaching classes from here. But why are you asking me this? Is everything okay? "Then Lily said to me that actually I am alone today can you walk with me to the bus stand? And then that day I went with Lily to the bus stand. After that Lily went home by bus and I went to my coaching class. But I was starting to get worried for Lily.

Will she have reached home well? This question started coming in my mind. So I texted Lily, "Have you reach home well; haven't you? After that she replied, "Yes dear, and thank you for your help." And from that day we started talking every day. Our friendship got stronger day by day. Lily asked me one day, "When will you invite me to your house? "Then I said, "Whenever you want". She replied, "Okay, then i will come to your house tomorrow". I said, Okay. The next day on 11th November, I fell ill. But when my phone rang, I saw that was Lily's call. I jumped out of the bed and picked up the phone, she asked me to give my address to the cab driver. After 5 minutes, I had gone to the cab stoppage and waited for her. After 2 minutes she came in front of me and smiling at me. Her smile was priceless, I couldn't describe her smile. She looked so cute while she was smiling. I couldn't take my eyes off her. Whole day we talked with each other on various topics and enjoyed our day. After lunch, she told me that she had to leave then because her home was too far from my house. The distance from my house to her house is approximately 25 KM. So I took her to our nearest bus stand and told her "bye bye". For me that day I spent a very peaceful day with her and couldn't forget about that day. Even after reaching home that day, we talked a lot. After 3 days I had gone to a party, where an unknown girl came in front of me and requested me to take a selfie with her. Only because she was younger than me I also agreed on her request. But when I sent all the photographs to Lily, she became very angry with me but when I asked her why you were angry with me. She replied me in an angry mood "why did you take photos with that nonsense girl?" meant she was feeling jealous. I told her why you were feeling jealous neither you were my best friend nor you were my girlfriend. Then from what position you were telling me. She had no reply. After thinking for few minutes she told me that she was angry only because I had not clicked any photo with her. After her reply, in my mind a question arose, "Was that really the reason or something or does she love me?" I didn't understand anything.

At that night a girl whose name was Jhanvi, she had a crush on me. She texted Lily through Instagram and warned her not to come close me. When Lily asked her, why? She replied, "Raj is only mine". Lily became very angry after seeing that message. She directly texted me and asked me, "Who the hell is Jhanvi?" I just told her that she was my just a normal friend nothing more. But after listening to her, I directly asked her, what is wrong with you Lily, why are you tensioning about this? Neither you are my best friend nor you are my Girlfriend then why?" Without giving any perfect answer of my question she told me "Nothing but I don't like her". Again this question came to my mind, "Is she loves me?"

After 7 days I told everything to jaan who was one of my closest friend. After observing everything she replied me with a smiley face "Duffer you love her. Why aren't you proposing her? And I am sure that Lily also loves you". But when I thought about that, I felt that, "Yes Jaan is absolutely right. I love Lily." There were many questions coming in my mind, if I propose her, she will reject me because I knew very well that she had been loved with a guy for 3 years and she couldn't forget him. And when she missed him, she used to cry. Our friendship could come to be strange, what I didn't want at all. Another major tension was that because of my profession, her life would be in danger. These kind of tensions were not allowing me propose to her. Then I decided to stop talking to her. I tried a lot not to talk to her but I could not stop myself. And after 2 hours I texted her and told her "Hi, what are you doing dear?" I failed to keep my decision, so that night I decided to go to Delhi, because I was very clear that if I stayed there for a few more days I would not be able to leave. So I planned to leave my place and go to Delhi. I told my friend, Jaan about that. Jaan told me that I should tell her what was on my heart. And I also wanted to tell her about my feelings but I was unable to tell. At that night when I was talking to her suddenly I thought maybe I should tell her everything. After a while I told her that "I think I love you." She was silent for a while. After that she told me, "Okay, I will not reject your proposal but I need some time to think about yourself." Then I told her, "Of course, please take your time because this is a decision which will decide your future happiness." As days were passing my tension level was growing with time. After 5 days I felt that maybe she must be feeling a bit awkward to rejecting me because it could have broken our friendship too. So, I thought of leaving from her life without knowing her so I started my packing. I wanted to go to Delhi, because my father's office headquarter was on Delhi. But Jaan told Lily everything that I was going to Delhi the next day. I didn't know that Jaan told her everything. After that Lily texted me and asked me, "Where are you going and why? I told you not to go anywhere". Then I replied her that, "I think you've got a misunderstanding and who told you I'm going somewhere." After 10 minutes, at 8:37 PM she told me that "I am accepting your proposal which you offered me few days ago." After reading that message from Lily, I just jumped out of bed, I was so happy that day. Till today my happiest day of my life is November 27th because that day I started a new journey with my Lily. Our relationship became stronger day by day. After 2 months, I got a message from headquarter that I had to go for a counter militancy operationThat day was the first day of my life after I entered service when I got worried about my life. I really didn't care about my life when Lily was not in my life but since Lily came into my life I really started caring about my life. In that operation, unfortunately a bullet hit my stomach, after that shot I was losing my consciousness. I was thinking only of Lily before I lost my senses. There was only one thing running through my mind, if something happened to me then what would happen with lily. Fortunately, I got proper treatment at the right time and that's why I survived. After some days, when I went to college she asked me when was your trip get over. I told her, "At yesterday night." Before leaving for the operation I told her that I was going on a trip so she told me "When did you come from the trip?" But from that day I started feeling scared how would Lily react if she found out about my profession. So I thought that she was my partner and so she had the right to know about my profession. So I decided to tell her everything. Next day at night I told her everything about my profession. After hearing everything she started crying. I asked, "What happen Lily? Why are you crying? " She replied me crying, "If you stay in this service then there will always be risk in your life which I don't want at all. Can you resign from your service for me? If something happens to you, then how will i survive?" And saying this she started crying again. I was really afraid when I saw her crying. Her tears were reflecting her love and care for me. That day I realised that Lily really loved me a lot. I couldn't see Lily's condition, so I told her, "Please don't cry dear, I am sending my resignation through mail but it will take some time." After few days my resignation letter was accepted officially.

After 2 months I got an invitation from Lily's family for an occasion. I was overjoyed after getting the invitation as this would be my first meeting at her house. But I was also a little nervous as I would meet her parents for the first time.

Finally the day came when I was going to meet her. That day I was too happy because I was too excited to meet her at her home. I promised her that I would reach your home before 9 AM, so I left from my house at 8 AM. That day I was driving the car and after 15 minutes I noticed a black car that was following me for a while, but I thought it was normal but after 5 minutes when I stopped my car to pick a call, I noticed that the black car also was stopped. I was feeling something not so good, so I called Bose and told her everything. After that again I started driving and took my car in different direction which was completely opposite from Lily's house. After a while when I was passing from a remote area they began to firing on my car with AK-47 and some other assault rifle. But my car was bullet proof so I was safe. But fortunately after 5 minutes of firing Bose and other team members reached there in time and rescued me. After that I had gone to Lily's colony and then I thought why shouldn't I do a prank with Lily? After that I called her and told her, "I am sorry Lily. I can't come to your house. Then Lily asked me in a low voice, why? Then I told her, "Some urgent work has come, which I have to do and that is very important. "And saying this I disconnected the call. I understood that Lily got very sad. But when I was in call with lily her mother saw me and just called her, "Lily..... Where are you, see who has come?" Hearing her mother's voice, lily came out and saw me and was run to me. When she saw me she became too much happy which was reflecting on her face. After that she told me, "Do you even know how much I was get scared?" Then I told her,

"Sorry dear, i just wanted to do a prank with you." After hearing this she replied, Okay.... No problem, but never do that again. "I told her, Okay dear.... That day I spent too much time with Lily. And that was too precious for me. Her mom dad was also too good. At her home I noticed a childhood photo of her which was hanging in a wall. Suddenly this thought came in my mind, Have I seen this photo anywhere? I was just thinking the whole day, "Where I see her, where...where... "A few days later, I remembered that I saw her in a bus journey a few years back. At that time also, I became crazy on seeing her. When I told her about this incident, she was just smiling quietly. I was so happy to see her smile. That was too peaceful. After a few days she told me, "I have told my mom about our relationship and she doesn't have any problem with our relationship. After listening this at first I was just shocked but later I realise that I was the most luckiest person of this planet.

Everything was going well. But once in the evening Bose came to my house and told me that I had a video of Lily. I told her 'Oh; But what kind of video', she told me please watch the video, I said 'ok'. After watching the video I was completely perplexed and I also got very angry. In that video, Lily was standing in the bus and a boy was touching her. The bus was full of passengers so she stood and did not feel any bad touch as she had high fever that day. I told Bose that I wanted complete information about that idiot in just 30 minutes, who did this. I told him to take permission from higher authority for arrest as it was a gang which used to make such videos and blackmail innocent girls. That night, Bose's team and I reached our destination where the entire gang lived. In 2 hours operation we caught all those who were involved in this crime, all of them were arrested and our team deleted all videos of different girls.

We have seen many good days and bad days in the journey of our relationship.

One day I told Lily that "Why don't you ever listen to me? I told you not to drink too much cold-drink but you are buying cold drinks every day which causes many problems in your health. I didn't talk to her that day. Next day when she came to college, she told me "Sorry, I will never buy or drink soft drinks" I replied that "I am not telling you not to consume such things, I am just telling you not to consume too much because it can lead to illness.

But our love for each other never decreased in this whole incident because we knew that a healthy relationship included both good and bad situations.

In this journey, many people tried hard to separate us but our bond became stronger. Our journey starts from a stranger then a friend then a secret keeper then my favourite friend then my best friend at last my partner, in this whole journey we faced many problems as well as we saw many beautiful things together. I wish and I pray to god that he always keep us together in a strong bond.

To be continue................